Dot and the Big Cat

by Lynn Maslen Kertell
pictures by Dana Sullivan

Scholastic Inc.

Copyright © 2015 by Lynn Maslen Kertell. All rights reserved. Published by Scholastic Inc. Publishers since 1920. Published by arrangement with Bob Books® Publications LLC. SCHOLASTIC and associated logos are trademarks and/or registered trademarks of Scholastic Inc. BOB BOOKS are trademarks and/or registered trademarks of Bob Books® Publications LLC.

Lexile® is a registered trademark of MetaMetrics Inc.

22 21 20 19   21 22 23 24

Printed in China 68
This edition first printing, August 2020

Dot met a dog.

The dog is fat.

Dot met a hen.

The hen is red.

Dot met a crab.

The crab is wet.

Dot met a cat.

The cat is big.

Run, Dot, run!

The End